LAKEWOOD SCHOOL LIBRARY

219303

E
TOM
Tompert, Ann
The silver whistle

DATE DUE			

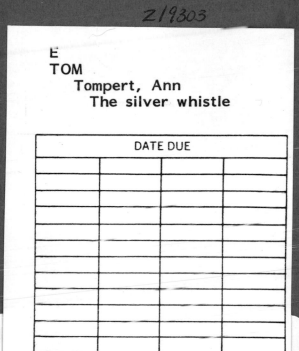

219303

LAKEWOOD SCHOOL LIBRARY

no S.L.

LAKEWOOD SCHOOL LIBRARY

The Silver Whistle

Ann Tompert ✦ Illustrated by Beth Peck

Macmillan Publishing Company   New York
Collier Macmillan Publishers   London

219303

2/89

Text copyright © 1988 by Ann Tompert. Illustrations copyright © 1988 by Beth Peck. All rights reserved. No part of this book may be reproduced or transmitted in any form or by any means, electronic or mechanical, including photocopying, recording, or by any information storage and retrieval system, without permission in writing from the Publisher.

Macmillan Publishing Company, 866 Third Avenue, New York, NY 10022. Collier Macmillan Canada, Inc.

Printed and bound in Japan. First American Edition.   10 9 8 7 6 5 4 3 2 1

The text of this book is set in 16 point Garamond No. 3. The illustrations are rendered in pen-and-ink with watercolor. Library of Congress Cataloging-in-Publication Data   Tompert, Ann.   The silver whistle/Ann Tompert; illustrated by Beth Peck.—1st American ed.   p.   cm.   Summary: Having generously aided the needy with money he'd earned to buy a silver whistle for a gift to the Christ Child on Christmas Eve, a Mexican boy approaches the manger in the cathedral in embarrassment, only to find that he has pleased the Baby Jesus after all.   ISBN 0-02-789160-7   [1. Christmas—Fiction. 2. Mexico—Fiction.] I. Peck, Beth, ill. II. Title.   PZ7.T598Si 1988 [E]—dc 19   88-1446 CIP AC

For Liza —A.T.

For Alan, my parents, Robert, and Judy—B.P.

The red rim of the sun was at the edge of the morning sky.

"Is it much farther?" Miguel asked for the hundredth time since they had left home just after midnight.

"Up and over this hill and down into the valley," said his father, "and we'll be there."

Miguel's father was almost lost in the jumble of clay pots, bowls, jars, mugs, and jugs that he was hauling. Miguel's mother carried his baby sister in a dark blue shawl slung across her back. And Miguel had a basket on his back, held with a strap across his forehead. In it were carefully packed the painted clay whistles in the shapes of birds and animals that his father had taught him to make.

Here and there on the many foot trails that twisted
around the steep mountains and through the narrow valleys,
Miguel could see other travelers. It was the day before
Christmas, and, as had been the custom for many years,
the people from the surrounding countryside were journeying
to town for a festival.

"Suppose Diego doesn't come," Miguel said.

"No one misses the greatest festival of the year," said
his father, "especially not Diego, the silversmith."

"But, son," said his mother, "you must not be
disappointed if he has sold the silver whistle by now."

Miguel's heart skipped a beat. From the moment he had seen it at the festival of San Pedro in August, he had known that he had to have the silver whistle. Since then he had worked hard making clay whistles to sell at the markets and festivals. He felt the leather pouch tied to his waist. All the pesos he had saved were in it. After selling his clay whistles today, he was sure he would have enough money to bargain for the silver one.

They had reached the top of the hill. In the valley below and tucked against the sides of the surrounding mountains, Miguel saw little pink and blue and yellow houses whose red-tiled roofs glowed in the morning sun. In the center of the valley was the plaza, filled with shops and stands. A magnificent cathedral towered over everything.

Tonight Miguel would carry the silver whistle in the Procession of Gifts at the cathedral. How proud he would feel! Such a wonderful gift surely would be put in the place of honor at the foot of the manger. And maybe, just maybe, it would happen as his grandfather had said. The Holy One would be so pleased with the gift that he would smile. Though how a statue made of wood could smile, Miguel did not know.

By the time Miguel's family arrived at the plaza, it was brimming with people. Little stands with awnings were springing up all over. The streets leading away from the plaza were filled, too. And paper streamers were fluttering everywhere.

Miguel glanced about the milling crowds. Maybe the silversmith hadn't come, after all. "Please, papa," he said, "may I look for Diego's stand now?"

"It's best you sell your whistles first," said his father. And he led the way past a group of men who were dancing to the music of a flute and drums.

Miguel lagged behind, still hoping to see Diego.

"Over here, Miguel," called his father. He had found a small space between a food stand and one filled with baskets.

Reluctantly, Miguel joined his father and mother, and the three of them carefully arranged their wares on reed mats under an awning.

It wasn't long before people were pressing on all sides, bargaining with Miguel's father, for he was the best potter for miles around.

Miguel was busy, too, and by late afternoon he had sold everything except a little yellow bird, the very first whistle he had ever made. It was an odd-looking creature with lumpy wings, a twisted beak, and a crooked tail. When he had tried to sell it, people had laughed at him. And so he tucked the little yellow bird in his pouch, rolled up his mat, and set out to find Diego.

"Don't forget your serape!" his mother called after him. "And don't be too long!"

Almost at once, Miguel was caught up in the excitement of the festival. One moment he was standing in front of a glassblower making a lantern from a blob of soft glass at the end of a tube. The next moment, he found himself beside a juggler. Then he was passing the huge fireworks castle that was to be set off after the Procession of Gifts.

Miguel was often tempted to loosen the strings of his leather pouch. There was a merry-go-round to ride and brightly colored, bird-shaped sweets to eat and sugarcane to chew. There were great copper pots to buy for his mother, leather sandals for his father, and a wooden doll for his sister. But Miguel resisted them all.

He was squeezing past a crowd watching a puppet show
when he bumped into a man who was trying to pull
a burro to its feet.

"Watch where you're going, stupid one!" shouted the
man. "Isn't it enough that I have this balky burro to put up
with?" He picked up a stick and struck the burro.

"Please, sir, don't," cried Miguel.

"This animal is no good," the man shouted, hitting the
burro again. "I'd sell her if I could find someone foolish
enough to buy her."

Miguel pulled out his pouch and cried, "I'll buy her. I'll buy her."

Minutes later, the burro's owner had disappeared into the crowd with all of Miguel's pesos. Only then did Miguel remember the silver whistle.

How stupid he was! What could he do with a balky burro? He could not march her in the Procession of Gifts. And he would not sell her unless he was sure she would be well treated. Would Diego trade the silver whistle for her?

"What a fine burro!" said a voice, interrupting Miguel's thoughts. A man, bent under the weight of years and the basket of serapes on his back, was stroking the burro's head.

"I am no longer young," he said. "How much better for me if I had a fine burro like this one." He eased the basket of serapes from his shoulders. "I have no money, but I can give you something fit for a young prince."

The man held up a white serape, on whose edges were woven red birds and flowers. It was the most beautiful serape Miguel had ever seen.

While Miguel wondered what to do, the burro nuzzled against the man's arm. The man whispered in her ear. The burro stood up. "It was meant to be," Miguel said. And he took the serape from the man. Surely Diego would trade the silver whistle for the serape.

By the time Miguel had helped the man arrange his serapes on the burro's back, the sun had settled behind the mountains and the torches were being lighted. The air had grown chilly. Miguel was glad his mother had reminded him to take his serape.

He went from stall to stall, asking about Diego. "Have you seen Diego, the silversmith?" he asked a woman in a flower stall.

"Oh, yes," she said. "His stall was next to mine. But he is gone now. Such beautiful things he had!"

"He has sold them all, then?" Miguel could not keep the panic from his voice.

"Not all," said the woman.

"The whistle? Did he sell the whistle?" Miguel asked.

Before she could answer, a small, barefoot boy wearing only a thin shirt ran to her. The boy shivered. She picked him up and wrapped him in her shawl.

Glancing around the stall, Miguel saw that the woman was very poor. A wave of defeat washed over him. Of all places, why had he stopped here? Maybe he could just pretend that everything was all right with this woman and her child. He could leave before he did something stupid.

A deep, racking cough shook the boy's body.

Miguel sighed. "For your son," he said, placing the white serape with its red-figured border beside her. Then he ran off into the darkness.

Miguel did not stop running until he neared the cathedral. Its great doors had been flung open wide. Thick crowds of people jostled about as they lined up for the Procession of Gifts. He caught a glimpse of his family. His father was carrying the beautiful Communion cup he had made. His mother was talking with a brown-robed monk.

Miguel tried to melt into the crowd, but his father saw him. "There he is!" Miguel's father shouted, and he worked his way, inch by inch, through the mob. The monk and Miguel's mother, carrying the baby, followed him.

"Did you get the silver whistle?" his father asked when they reached Miguel.

"No, papa." And with words tumbling one over the other, he told them about the burro and the serape seller and the flower woman with her small son. He hardly paused for breath, afraid that the threatening tears would spill over.

"What you have done is good, son," said his mother.

"But now I have nothing for the Infant," said Miguel.

"Do you still have your yellow bird?" asked his father.

Miguel nodded and slowly removed it from his pouch.

The monk took the misshapen little bird from him and studied it for a moment. "I think the Holy One would be most pleased with this bird," he said.

Miguel's father nodded. "You can put it beside my cup."

Shortly after the monk had left them, the procession started through the cathedral doors, and they joined the line. Anger filled Miguel. How could his father expect him to present such an ugly gift to the Infant? He tried to hold the yellow bird so that no one could see it. People were probably nudging each other and winking. How different this was from the way he had dreamed it all these months!

Slowly the line flowed into the cathedral, where shadows danced in the flickering candlelight. Down the main aisle Miguel moved. He felt more and more miserable with each step.

At last he reached the Nativity scene, but he could not bear to look at the manger where the Infant lay. His eyes darted about frantically. Where could he hide his ugly gift? He spied a sombrero. He reached out to tuck the yellow bird under its brim, but a hand closed over his. Miguel looked up. The hand belonged to the monk, who took the yellow bird from Miguel and put it tenderly in the place of honor at the foot of the manger.

Tears sprang into Miguel's eyes. He was so tired and disappointed and ashamed. He must take the bird back and run and hide it where no one would ever find it. Then, through tear-blurred eyes, he saw a beautiful golden bird shimmering in the flickering candlelight. That bird wasn't his. Or was it?

Miguel's glance strayed to the Infant's face. He caught his breath. His heart pounded. It was happening just as his grandfather had said it would. The Holy One was pleased with his gift. Was that not a smile on his face?